Writing 21

RICHARD BRAUTIGAN

IN
WATERMELON
SUGAR

A Delta Book

A DELTA BOOK
Published by Dell Publishing Co., Inc.
750 Third Avenue
New York, N.Y. 10017
This book was first published by Four Seasons
Foundation in its Writing series edited
by Donald Allen

Cover photograph by Edmund Shea

Manufactured in the United States of America
Fourth printing

Book One:
In Watermelon Sugar

In Watermelon Sugar

IN WATERMELON SUGAR the deeds were done and done again as my life is done in watermelon sugar. I'll tell you about it because I am here and you are distant.

Wherever you are, we must do the best we can. It is so far to travel, and we have nothing here to travel, except watermelon sugar. I hope this works out.

I live in a shack near iDEATH. I can see iDEATH out the window. It is beautiful. I can also see it with my eyes closed and touch it. Right now it is cold and turns like something in the hand of a child. I do not know what that thing could be.

There is a delicate balance in iDEATH. It suits us.

The shack is small but pleasing and comfortable as my life and made from pine, watermelon sugar and stones as just about everything here is.

Our lives we have carefully constructed from watermelon sugar and then travelled to the length of our dreams, along roads lined with pines and stones.

I have a bed, a chair, a table and a large chest that I keep my things in. I have a lantern that burns watermelontrout oil at night.

That is something else. I'll tell you about it later. I have a gentle life.

1

I go to the window and look out again. The sun is shining at the long edge of a cloud. It is Tuesday and the sun is golden.

I can see piney woods and the rivers that flow from those piney woods. The rivers are cold and clear and there are trout in the rivers.

Some of the rivers are only a few inches wide.

I know a river that is half-an-inch wide. I know because I measured it and sat beside it for a whole day. It started raining in the middle of the afternoon. We call everything a river here. We're that kind of people.

I can see fields of watermelons and the rivers that flow through them. There are many bridges in the piney woods and in the fields of watermelons. There is a bridge in front of this shack.

Some of the bridges are made of wood, old and stained silver like rain, and some of the bridges are made of stone gathered from a great distance and built in the order of that distance, and some of the bridges are made of watermelon sugar. I like those bridges best.

We make a great many things out of watermelon sugar here —I'll tell you about it—including this book being written near iDEATH.

All this will be gone into, travelled in watermelon sugar.

2

Margaret

THIS MORNING there was a knock at the door. I could tell who it was by the way they knocked, and I heard them coming across the bridge.

They stepped on the only board that makes any noise. They always step on it. I have never been able to figure this out. I have thought a great deal about why they always step on that same board, how they cannot miss it, and now they stood outside my door, knocking.

I did not acknowledge their knocking because I just wasn't interested. I did not want to see them. I knew what they would be about and did not care for it.

Finally they stopped knocking and went back across the bridge and they, of course, stepped on the same board: a long board with the nails not lined up right, built years ago and no way to fix it, and then they were gone, and the board was silent.

I can walk across the bridge hundreds of times without stepping on that board, but Margaret always steps on it.

3

My Name

I GUESS YOU ARE KIND OF CURIOUS as to who I am, but I am one of those who do not have a regular name. My name depends on you. Just call me whatever is in your mind.

If you are thinking about something that happened a long time ago: Somebody asked you a question and you did not know the answer.

That is my name.

Perhaps it was raining very hard.

That is my name.

Or somebody wanted you to do something. You did it. Then they told you what you did was wrong—"Sorry for the mistake,"—and you had to do something else.

That is my name.

Perhaps it was a game that you played when you were a child or something that came idly into your mind when you were old and sitting in a chair near the window.

That is my name.

Or you walked someplace. There were flowers all around.

That is my name.

Perhaps you stared into a river. There was somebody near you who loved you. They were about to touch you. You could feel this before it happened. Then it happened.

That is my name.

Or you heard someone calling from a great distance. Their voice was almost an echo.

That is my name.

Perhaps you were lying in bed, almost ready to go to sleep and you laughed at something, a joke unto yourself, a good way to end the day.

That is my name.

Or you were eating something good and for a second forgot what you were eating, but still went on, knowing it was good.

That is my name.

Perhaps it was around midnight and the fire tolled like a bell inside the stove.

That is my name.

Or you felt bad when she said that thing to you. She could have told it to someone else: Somebody who was more familiar with her problems.

That is my name.

Perhaps the trout swam in the pool but the river was only eight inches wide and the moon shone on iDEATH and the watermelon fields glowed out of proportion, dark and the moon seemed to rise from every plant.

That is my name.

And I wish Margaret would leave me alone.

Fred

A LITTLE WHILE after Margaret left, Fred came by. He was not involved with the bridge. He only used it to get to my shack. He had nothing else to do with the bridge. He only walked across it to get to my place.

He just opened the door and came in. "Hi," he said. "What's up?"

"Nothing much," I said. "Just working away here."

"I just came from the Watermelon Works," Fred said. "I want you to go down there tomorrow morning with me. I want to show you something about the plank press."

"All right," I said.

"Good," he said. "I'll see you tonight at dinner down at iDEATH. I hear Pauline is going to cook dinner tonight. That means we'll have something good. I'm a little tired of Al's cooking. The vegetables are always overdone, and I'm tired of carrots, too. If I eat another carrot this week I'll scream."

"Yeah, Pauline's a good cook," I said. I wasn't really too much interested in food at the time. I wanted to get back to my work, but Fred is my buddy. We've had a lot of good times together.

Fred had something strange-looking sticking out of the pocket of his overalls. I was curious about it. It looked like something I had never seen before.

6

"What's that in your pocket, Fred?"

"I found it today coming through the woods up from the Watermelon Works. I don't know what it is myself. I've never seen anything like it before. What do you think it is?"

He took it out of his pocket and handed it to me. I didn't know how to hold it. I tried to hold it like you would hold a flower and a rock at the same time.

"How do you hold it?" I said.

"I don't know. I don't know anything about it."

"It looks like one of those things inBOIL and his gang used to dig up down at the Forgotten Works. I've never seen anything like it," I said, and gave it back to Fred.

"I'll show it to Charley," he said. "Maybe Charley will know. He knows about everything there is."

"Yeah, Charley knows a lot," I said.

"Well, I guess I had better be going," Fred said. He put the thing back in his overalls. "I'll see you at dinner," he said.

"OK."

Fred went out the door. He crossed the bridge without stepping on that board Margaret always steps on and couldn't miss if the bridge were seven miles wide.

Charley's Idea

AFTER FRED LEFT it felt good to get back to writing again, to dip my pen in watermelonseed ink and write upon these sheets of sweet-smelling wood made by Bill down at the shingle factory.

Here is a list of the things that I will tell you about in this book. There's no use saving it until later. I might as well tell you now where you're at—

1: iDEATH. (A good place.)

2: Charley (My friend.)

3: The tigers and how they lived and how beautiful they were and how they died and how they talked to me while they ate my parents, and how I talked back to them and how they stopped eating my parents, though it did not help my parents any, nothing could help them by then, and we talked for a long time and one of the tigers helped me with my arithmetic, then they told me to go away while they finished eating my parents, and I went away. I returned later that night to burn the shack down. That's what we did in those days.

4: The Statue of Mirrors.

5: Old Chuck.

6: The long walks I take at night. Sometimes I stand for hours at a single place, without hardly moving. (I've had the wind stop in my hand.)

7 :   The Watermelon Works.
8 :   Fred. (My buddy.)
9 :   The baseball park.
10 :   The aqueduct.
11 :   Doc Edwards and the schoolteacher.
12 :   The beautiful trout hatchery at iDEATH and how it was built and the things that happen there. (It's a swell place for dancing.)
13 :   The Tomb Crew, the Shaft and the Shaft Gallows.
14 :   A waitress.
15 :   Al, Bill, others.
16 :   The town.
17 :   The sun and how it changes. (Very interesting.)
18 :   inBOIL and that gang of his and the place where they used to dig, the Forgotten Works, and all the terrible things they did, and what happened to them, and how quiet and nice things are around here now that they are dead.
19 :   Conversations and things that happen here day to day. (Work, baths, breakfast and dinner.)
20 :   Margaret and that other girl who carried the lantern at night and never came close.
21 :   All of our statues and the places where we bury our dead, so that they are forever with light coming out of their tombs.
22 :   My life lived in watermelon sugar. (There must be worse lives.)
23 :   Pauline. (She is my favorite. You'll see.)
24 :   And this the twenty-fourth book written in 171 years. Last month Charley said to me, "You don't seem to like making statues or doing anything else. Why don't you write a book?

"The last one was written thirty-five years ago. It's about time somebody wrote another book."

Then he scratched his head and said, "Gee, I remember it was written thirty-five years ago, but I can't remember what it was about. There used to be a copy of it in the sawmill."

"Do you know who wrote it?" I said.

"No," he said. "But he was like you. He didn't have a regular name."

I asked him what the other books were about, the twenty-three previous ones, and he said that he thought one of them was about owls.

"Yeah, it was about owls, and then there was a book about pine needles, very boring, and then there was one about the Forgotten Works, theories on how it got started and where it came from.

"The guy who wrote the book, his name was Mike, he took a long trip into the Forgotten Works. He went in maybe a hundred miles and was gone for weeks. He went beyond those high Piles we can see on clear days. He said that there were Piles beyond those that were even higher.

"He wrote a book about his journey into the Forgotten Works. It wasn't a bad book, a lot better than the books we find in the Forgotten Works. Those are terrible books.

"He said he was lost for days and came across things that were two miles long and green. He refused to furnish any other details about them, even in his book. Just said they were two miles long and green.

"That's his tomb down by that statue of a frog."

"I know that tomb well," I said. "He has blond hair and he's wearing a pair of rust-colored overalls."

"Yeah, that's him," Charley said.

Sundown

AFTER I FINISHED WRITING for the day it was close to sundown and dinner would be ready soon down at iDEATH.

I looked forward to seeing Pauline and eating what she would cook and seeing her at dinner and maybe I would see her after dinner. We might go for a long walk, maybe along the aqueduct.

Then maybe we would go to her shack for the night or stay at iDEATH or come back up here, if Margaret wouldn't knock the door down the next time she came by.

The sun was going down over the Piles in the Forgotten Works. They turned back far beyond memory and glowed in the sundown.

The Gentle Cricket

I WENT OUT AND STOOD on the bridge for a while and looked down at the river below. It was three feet wide. There were a couple of statues standing in the water. One of them was my mother. She was a good woman. I made it five years ago.

The other statue was a cricket. I did not make that one. Somebody else made it a long time ago in the time of the tigers. It is a very gentle statue.

I like my bridge because it is made of all things: wood and the distant stones and gentle planks of watermelon sugar.

I walked down to iDEATH through a long cool twilight that passed like a tunnel over me. I lost sight of iDEATH when I passed into the piney woods and the trees smelled cold and they were growing steadily darker.

Lighting the Bridges

I LOOKED UP through the pines and saw the evening star. It glowed a welcoming red from the sky, for that is the color of our stars here. They are always that color.

I counted a second evening star on the opposite side of the sky, not as imposing but just as beautiful as the one that arrived first.

I came upon the real bridge and the abandoned bridge. They were side by side across a river. Trout were jumping in the river. A trout about twenty inches long jumped. I thought it was a rather nice fish. I knew I would remember it for a long time.

I saw somebody coming up the road. It was Old Chuck coming up from iDEATH to light the lanterns on the real bridge and the abandoned bridge. He was walking slowly because he is a very old man.

Some say that he is too old to light the bridges and that he should just stay down at iDEATH and take it easy. But Old Chuck likes to light the lanterns and come back in the morning and put them out.

Old Chuck says that everybody should have something to do and lighting those bridges is his thing to do. Charley agrees with him. "Let Old Chuck light the bridges if he feels like it. It keeps him out of mischief."

13

This is a kind of joke because Old Chuck must be ninety years old if he's a day and mischief has passed far beyond him, moving at the speed of decades.

Old Chuck has bad eyes and did not see me until he was almost on top of me. I waited for him. "Hello, Chuck," I said.

"Good evening," he said. "I've come to light the bridges. How are you this evening? I've come to light the bridges. Beautiful evening, isn't it?"

"Yes," I said. "Lovely."

Old Chuck went over to the abandoned bridge and took a six-inch match out of his overalls and lit the lantern on the iDEATH side of the bridge. The abandoned bridge has been that way since the time of the tigers.

In those days two tigers were trapped on the bridge and killed and then the bridge was set on fire. The fire only destroyed part of the bridge.

The bodies of the tigers fell into the river and you can still see their bones lying on the bottom in the sandy places and lodged in the rocks and scattered here and there: small bones and rib bones and part of a skull.

There is a statue in the river alongside the bones. It is the statue of somebody who was killed by the tigers a long time ago. Nobody knows who they were.

They never repaired the bridge and now it is the abandoned bridge. There is a lantern at each end of the bridge. Old Chuck lights them every evening, though some people say he is too old.

The real bridge is made entirely of pine. It is a covered bridge and always dark inside like an ear. The lanterns are in the shape of faces.

One face is that of a beautiful child and the other face is that of a trout. Old Chuck lit the lanterns with the long matches from his overalls.

The lanterns on the abandoned bridge are tigers.

"I'll walk with you down to iDEATH," I said.

"Oh no," Old Chuck said. "I'm too slow. You'll be late for

14

dinner."

"What about you?" I said.

"I've already eaten. Pauline gave me something to eat just before I left."

"What are we having for dinner?" I said.

"No," Old Chuck said, smiling. "Pauline told me if I met you on the road not to tell you what the dinner is tonight. She made me promise."

"That Pauline," I said.

"She made me promise," he said.

iDEATH

IT WAS ABOUT DARK when I arrived at iDEATH. The two evening
stars were now shining side by side. The smaller one had moved
over to the big one. They were very close now, almost touching,
and then they went together and became one very large star.

I don't know if things like that are fair or not.

There were lights on down at iDEATH. I watched them as I
came down the hill out of the woods. They looked warm, calling
and cheery.

Just before I arrived at iDEATH, it changed. iDEATH's like that:
always changing. It's for the best. I walked up the stairs to the
front porch and opened the door and went in.

I walked across the living room toward the kitchen. There
was nobody in the room, nobody sitting on the couches along
the river. That's where people usually gather in the room or they
stand in the trees by the big rocks, but there was nobody there
either. There were many lanterns shining along the river and
in the trees. It was very close to dinner.

When I got on the other side of the room, I could smell something good coming out of the kitchen. I left the room and walked
down the hall that follows beneath the river. I could hear the
river above me, flowing out of the living room. The river
sounded fine.

16

The hall was as dry as anything and I could smell good things coming up the hall from the kitchen.

Almost everybody was in the kitchen: that is, those who take their meals at iDEATH. Charley and Fred were talking about something. Pauline was just getting ready to serve dinner. Everybody was sitting down. She was happy to see me. "Hi, stranger," she said.

"What's for dinner?" I said.

"Stew," she said. "The way you like it."

"Great," I said.

She gave me a nice smile and I sat down. Pauline was wearing a new dress and I could see the pleasant outlines of her body. The dress had a low front and I could see the delicate curve of her breasts. I was quite pleased by everything. The dress smelled sweet because it was made from watermelon sugar.

"How's the book coming?" Charley said.

"Fine," I said. "Just fine."

"I hope it's not about pine needles," he said.

Pauline served me first. She gave me a great big helping of stew. Everybody was aware of me being served first and the size of the helping, and everybody smiled, for they knew what it meant, and they were happy for the thing that was going on.

Most of them did not like Margaret any more. Almost everybody thought that she had conspired with inBOIL and that gang of his, though there had never been any real evidence.

"This stew really tastes good," Fred said. He put a big spoonful of stew in his mouth, almost spilling some on his overalls. "Ummmm—good," he repeated and then said under his breath, "A lot better than carrots."

Al almost heard him. He looked hard for a second over at Fred, but he didn't quite catch it because he relaxed then and said, "It certainly is, Fred."

Pauline laughed slightly, for she had heard Fred's comment and I gave her a look as if to say: Don't laugh too hard, deary. You know how Al is about his cooking.

Pauline nodded understandingly.

"Just as long as it isn't about pine needles," Charley repeated, though a good ten minutes had passed since he'd said anything and that had been about pine needles, too.

The Tigers

AFTER DINNER Fred said that he would do the dishes. Pauline said oh no, but Fred insisted by actually starting to clear the table. He picked up some spoons and plates, and that settled it.

Charley said that he thought he would go in the living room and sit by the river and smoke a pipe. Al yawned. The other guys said that they would do other things, and went off to do them.

And then Old Chuck came in.

"What took you so long?" Pauline said.

"I decided to rest by the river. I fell asleep and had a long dream about the tigers. I dreamt they were back again."

"Sounds horrible," Pauline said. She shivered and kind of drew her shoulders in like a bird and put her hands on them.

"No, it was all right," Old Chuck said. He sat down in a chair. It took him a long time to sit down and then it was as if the chair had grown him, he was in so close.

"This time they were different," he said. "They played musical instruments and went for long walks in the moon.

"They stopped and played by the river. Their instruments looked nice. They sang, too. You remember how beautiful their voices were."

Pauline shivered again.

"Yes," I said. "They had beautiful voices but I never heard them singing."

"They were singing in my dream. I remember the music but I can't remember the words. They were good songs, too, and there was nothing frightening about them. Perhaps I am an old man," he said.

"No, they had beautiful voices," I said.

"I liked their songs," he said. "Then I woke up and it was cold. I could see the lanterns on the bridges. Their songs were like the lanterns, burning oil."

"I was a little worried about you," Pauline said.

"No," he said. "I sat down in the grass and leaned up against a tree and fell asleep and had a long dream about the tigers, and they sang songs but I can't remember the words. Their instruments were nice, too. They looked like the lanterns."

Old Chuck's voice slowed down. His body kept relaxing until it seemed as if he had always been in that chair, his arms gently resting on watermelon sugar.

More Conversation at iDEATH

PAULINE AND I went into the living room and sat down on a couch in the grove of trees by the big pile of rocks. There were lanterns all around us.

I took her hand in mine. Her hand had a lot of strength gained through the process of gentleness and that strength made my hand feel secure, but there was a certain excitement, too.

She sat very close to me. I could feel the warmth of her body through her dress. In my mind the warmth was the same color as her dress, a kind of golden.

"How's the book coming along?" she said.

"Fine," I said.

"What's it about?" she said.

"Oh, I don't know," I said.

"Is it a secret?" she said, smiling.

"No," I said.

"Is it a romance like some of the books from the Forgotten Works?"

"No," I said. "It's not like those books."

"I remember when I was a child," she said. "We used to burn those books for fuel. There were so many of them. They burned for a long time, but there aren't that many now."

"No, it's just a book," I said.

"All right," she said. "I'll get off you, but you can't blame a person for being curious. Nobody has written a book here for so long. Certainly not in my lifetime."

Fred came in from washing the dishes. He saw us up in the trees. Lanterns illuminated us.

"Hello, up there," he yelled.

"Hi," we shouted down.

Fred walked up to us, crossing a little river that flowed into the main river at iDEATH. He came across a small metal bridge that rang out his footsteps. I believe that bridge was found in the Forgotten Works by inBOIL. He brought it down here and put it in.

"Thanks for doing the dishes," Pauline said.

"My pleasure," Fred said. "I'm sorry to bother you people, but I just thought I would come up and remind you about meeting me down at the plank press tomorrow morning. There's something I want to show you down there."

"I haven't forgotten," I said. "What's it about?"

"I'll show you tomorrow."

"Good."

"That's all I wanted to say. I know you people have a lot to talk about, so I'll go now. That certainly was a good dinner, Pauline."

"Do you still have that thing you showed me today?" I said. "I'd like Pauline to see it."

"What thing?" Pauline said.

"Something Fred found in the woods today."

"No, I don't have it," Fred said. "I left it in my shack. I'll show it to you tomorrow at breakfast."

"What is it?" Pauline said.

"We don't know what it is," I said.

"Yeah, it's a strange-looking thing," Fred said. "It's like one of those things from the Forgotten Works."

"Oh," Pauline said.

"Well, anyway, I'll show it to you tomorrow at breakfast."

22

"Good," she said. "I look forward to seeing it. Whatever it is. Sounds pretty mysterious."

"OK, then," Fred said. "I'll be going now. Just wanted to remind you about seeing me tomorrow at the plank press. It's kind of important."

"Don't feel as if you should rush off," I said. "Join us for a while. Sit down."

"No, no, no. Thank you, anyway," Fred said. "There's something I have to do up at my shack."

"OK," I said.

"Good-bye."

"Thanks again for doing the dishes," Pauline said.

"Think nothing of it."

A Lot of Good Nights

IT WAS NOW GETTING LATE and Pauline and I went down to say good night to Charley. We could barely see him sitting down on his couch, near the statues that he likes and the place where he builds a small fire to warm himself on cold nights.

Bill had joined him and they were sitting there together, talking with great interest about something. Bill was waving his arms in the air to show a part of the conversation.

"We came down to say good night," I said, interrupting them.

"Oh, hi," Charley said. "Yeah, good night. I mean, how are you people doing?"

"OK," I said.

"That was a wonderful dinner," Bill said.

"Yeah, that was really fine," Charley said. "Good stew."

"Thank you."

"See you tomorrow," I said.

"Are you going to spend the night here at iDEATH?" Charley said.

"No," I said. "I'm going to spend the night with Pauline."

"That's good," Charley said.

"Good night."

"Good night."

"Good night."

"Good night."

Vegetables

PAULINE'S SHACK was about a mile from iDEATH. She doesn't spend much time there. It's beyond the town. There are about 375 of us here in watermelon sugar.

A lot of people live in the town, but some live in shacks at other places, and there are of course we who live at iDEATH.

There were just a few lights on in the town, other than the street lamps. Doc Edwards' light was on. He always has a lot of trouble sleeping at night. The schoolteacher's light was on, too. He was probably working on a lesson for the children.

We stopped on the bridge across the river. There were pale green lanterns on the bridge. They were in the shape of human shadows. Pauline and I kissed. Her mouth was moist and cool. Perhaps because of the night.

I heard a trout jump in the river, a late jumper. The trout made a narrow doorlike splash. There was a statue nearby. The statue was of a gigantic bean. That's right, a bean.

Somebody a long time ago liked vegetables and there are twenty or thirty statues of vegetables scattered here and there in watermelon sugar.

There is the statue of an artichoke near the shingle factory and a ten-foot carrot near the trout hatchery at iDEATH and a head of lettuce near the school and a bunch of onions near the entrance to the Forgotten Works and there are other vegetable statues near people's shacks and a rutabaga by the ball park.

A little ways from my shack there is the statue of a potato. I don't particularly care for it, but a long time ago somebody loved vegetables.

I once asked Charley if he knew who it was, but he said he didn't have the slightest idea. "Must have really liked vegetables, though," Charley'd said.

"Yeah," I'd said. "There's the statue of a potato right near my shack."

We continued up the road to Pauline's place. We passed by the Watermelon Works. It was silent and dark. Tomorrow morning it would be filled with light and activity. We could see the aqueduct. It was a long long shadow now.

We came to another bridge across a river. There were the usual lanterns on the bridge and statues in the river. There were a dozen or so pale lights coming up from the bottom of the river. They were tombs.

We stopped.

"The tombs look nice tonight," Pauline said.

"Certainly do," I said.

"There are mostly children here, aren't there?"

"Yes," I said.

"They're really beautiful tombs," Pauline said.

Moths fluttered above the light that came out of the river from the tombs below. There were five or six moths fluttering over each tomb.

Suddenly a big trout jumped out of the water above a tomb and got one of the moths. The other moths scattered and then came back again, and the same trout jumped again and got another moth. He was a smart old trout.

The trout did not jump any more and the moths fluttered peacefully above the light coming from the tombs.

26

Margaret Again

"How's MARGARET taking all this?" Pauline said.

"I don't know," I said.

"Is she hurt or mad or what? Do you know how she feels?" Pauline said. "Has she talked to you about it since you told her? She hasn't talked to me at all. I saw her yesterday near the Watermelon Works. I said hello but she walked past me without saying anything. She seemed terribly upset."

"I don't know how she feels," I said.

"I thought she'd be at iDEATH tonight, but she wasn't there," Pauline said. "I don't know why I thought she'd be there. I just had a feeling but I was wrong. Have you seen her?"

"No," I said.

"I wonder where she's staying," Pauline said.

"I think she's staying with her brother."

"I feel bad about this. Margaret and I were such good friends. All the years we've spent together at iDEATH," Pauline said. "We were almost like sisters. I'm sorry that things had to work out this way, but there was nothing we could do about it."

"The heart is something else. Nobody knows what's going to happen," I said.

"You're right," Pauline said.

She stopped and kissed me. Then we crossed over the bridge to her shack.

Pauline's Shack

PAULINE'S SHACK is made entirely of watermelon sugar, except the door that is a good-looking grayish-stained pine with a stone doorknob.

Even the windows are made of watermelon sugar. A lot of windows here are made of sugar. It's very hard to tell the difference between sugar and glass, the way sugar is used by Carl the windowmaker. It's just a thing that depends on who is doing it. It's a delicate art and Carl has it.

Pauline lit a lantern. It smelled fragrant burning with watermelontrout oil. We have a way here also of mixing watermelon and trout to make a lovely oil for our lanterns. We use it for all our lighting purposes. It has a gentle fragrance to it, and makes a good light.

Pauline's shack is very simple as all our shacks are simple. Everything was in its proper place. Pauline uses the shack just to get away from iDEATH for a few hours or a night if she feels like it.

All of us who stay at iDEATH have shacks to visit whenever we feel like it. I spend more time at my shack than anybody else. I usually just sleep one night a week at iDEATH. I of course take most of my meals there. We who do not have regular names spend a lot of time by ourselves. It suits us.

"Well, here we are," Pauline said. She looked beautiful in the light of the lantern. Her eyes sparkled.

"Please come here," I said. She came over to me and I kissed her mouth and then I touched her breasts. They felt so smooth and firm. I put my hand down the front of her dress.

"That feels good," she said.

"Let's try some more," I said.

"That would be good," she said.

We went over and lay upon her bed. I took her dress off. She had nothing on underneath. We did that for a while. Then I got up and took off my overalls and lay back down beside her.

A Love, a Wind

WE MADE a long and slow love. A wind came up and the windows trembled slightly, the sugar set fragilely ajar by the wind.

I liked Pauline's body and she said that she liked mine, too, and we couldn't think of anything to say.

The wind suddenly stopped and Pauline said, "What's that?"

"It's the wind."

The Tigers Again

AFTER MAKING LOVE we talked about the tigers. It was Pauline who started it. She was lying warmly beside me, and she wanted to talk about the tigers. She said that Old Chuck's dream got her thinking about them.

"I wonder why they could speak our language," she said.

"No one knows," I said. "But they could speak it. Charley says maybe we were tigers a long time ago and changed but they didn't. I don't know. It's an interesting idea, though."

"I never heard their voices," Pauline said. "I was just a child and there were only a few tigers left, old ones, and they barely came out of the hills. They were too old to be dangerous, and they were hunted all the time.

"I was six years old when they killed the last one. I remember the hunters bringing it to iDEATH. There were hundreds of people with them. The hunters said they had killed it up in the hills that day, and it was the last tiger.

"They brought the tiger to iDEATH and everybody came with them. They covered it with wood and soaked the wood down with watermelontrout oil. Gallons and gallons of it. I remember people threw flowers on the pile and stood around crying because it was the last tiger.

"Charley took a match and lit the fire. It burned with a great

31

orange glow for hours and hours, and black smoke poured up into the air.

"It burned until there was nothing left but ashes, and then the men began right then and there building the trout hatchery at iDEATH, right over the spot where the tiger had been burned. It's hard to think of that now when you're down there dancing.

"I guess you remember all this," Pauline said. "You were there, too. You were standing beside Charley."

"That's right," I said. "They had beautiful voices."

"I never heard them" she said.

"Perhaps that was for the best," I said.

"Maybe you're right," she said. "Tigers," and was soon fast asleep in my arms. Her sleep tried to become my arm, and then my body, but I wouldn't let it because I was suddenly very restless.

I got up and put on my overalls and went for one of the long walks I take at night.

Arithmetic

THE NIGHT WAS COOL and the stars were red. I walked down by the Watermelon Works. That's where we process the watermelons into sugar. We take the juice from the watermelons and cook it down until there's nothing left but sugar, and then we work it into the shape of this thing that we have: our lives.

I sat down on a couch by the river. Pauline had gotten me thinking about the tigers. I sat there and thought about them, how they killed and ate my parents.

We lived together in a shack by the river. My father raised watermelons and my mother baked bread. I was going to school. I was nine years old and having trouble with arithmetic.

One morning the tigers came in while we were eating breakfast and before my father could grab a weapon they killed him and they killed my mother. My parents didn't even have time to say anything before they were dead. I was still holding the spoon from the mush I was eating.

"Don't be afraid," one of the tigers said. "We're not going to hurt you. We don't hurt children. Just sit there where you are and we'll tell you a story."

One of the tigers started eating my mother. He bit her arm off and started chewing on it. "What kind of story would you like to hear? I know a good story about a rabbit."

"I don't want to hear a story," I said.

"OK," the tiger said, and he took a bite out of my father. I sat there for a long time with the spoon in my hand, and then I put it down.

"Those were my folks," I said, finally.

"We're sorry," one of the tigers said. "We really are."

"Yeah," the other tiger said. "We wouldn't do this if we didn't have to, if we weren't absolutely forced to. But this is the only way we can keep alive."

"We're just like you," the other tiger said. "We speak the same language you do. We think the same thoughts, but we're tigers."

"You could help me with my arithmetic," I said.

"What's that?" one of the tigers said.

"My arithmetic."

"Oh, your arithmetic."

"Yeah."

"What do you want to know?" one of the tigers said.

"What's nine times nine?"

"Eighty-one," a tiger said.

"What's eight times eight?"

"Fifty-six," a tiger said.

I asked them half a dozen other questions: six times six, seven times four, etc. I was having a lot of trouble with arithmetic. Finally the tigers got bored with my questions and told me to go away.

"OK," I said. "I'll go outside."

"Don't go too far," one of the tigers said. "We don't want anyone to come up here and kill us."

"OK."

They both went back to eating my parents. I went outside and sat down by the river. "I'm an orphan," I said.

I could see a trout in the river. He swam directly at me and then he stopped right where the river ends and the land begins. He stared at me.

"What do you know about anything?" I said to the trout.

That was before I went to live at iDEATH.

After about an hour or so the tigers came outside and stretched and yawned.

"It's a nice day," one of the tigers said.

"Yeah," the other tiger said. "Beautiful."

"We're awfully sorry we had to kill your parents and eat them. Please try to understand. We tigers are not evil. This is just a thing we have to do."

"All right," I said. "And thanks for helping me with my arithmetic."

"Think nothing of it."

The tigers left.

I went over to iDEATH and told Charley that the tigers had eaten my parents.

"What a shame," he said.

"The tigers are so nice. Why do they have to go and do things like that?" I said.

"They can't help themselves," Charley said. "I like the tigers, too. I've had a lot of good conversations with them. They're very nice and have a good way of stating things, but we're going to have to get rid of them. Soon."

"One of them helped me with my arithmetic."

"They're very helpful," Charley said. "But they're dangerous. What are you going to do now?"

"I don't know," I said.

"How would you like to stay here at iDEATH?" Charley said.

"That sounds good," I said.

"Fine. Then it's settled," Charley said.

That night I went back to the shack and set fire to it. I didn't take anything with me and went to live at iDEATH. That was twenty years ago, though it seems like it was only yesterday: What's eight times eight?

She Was

FINALLY I STOPPED THINKING about the tigers and started back to Pauline's shack. I would think about the tigers another day. There would be many.

I wanted to stay the night with Pauline. I knew that she would be beautiful in her sleep, waiting for me to return. She was.

A Lamb at False Dawn

PAULINE BEGAN TALKING in her sleep at false dawn from under the watermelon covers. She told a little story about a lamb going for a walk.

"The lamb sat down in the flowers," she said. "The lamb was all right," and that was the end of the story.

Pauline often talks in her sleep. Last week she sang a little song. I forget how it went.

I put my hand on her breast. She stirred in her sleep. I took my hand off her breast and she was quiet again.

She felt very good in bed. There was a nice sleepy smell coming from her body. Perhaps that is where the lamb sat down.

The Watermelon Sun

I woke up before Pauline and put on my overalls. A crack of gray sun shone through the window and lay quietly on the floor. I went over and put my foot in it, and then my foot was gray.

I looked out the window and across the fields and piney woods and the town to the Forgotten Works. Everything was touched with gray: Cattle grazing in the fields and the roofs of the shacks and the big Piles in the Forgotten Works all looked like dust. The very air itself was gray.

We have an interesting thing with the sun here. It shines a different color every day. No one knows why this is, not even Charley. We grow the watermelons in different colors the best we can.

This is how we do it: Seeds gathered from a gray watermelon picked on a gray day and then planted on a gray day will make more gray watermelons.

It is really very simple. The colors of the days and the watermelons go like this—

Monday: red watermelons.
Tuesday: golden watermelons.
Wednesday: gray watermelons.
Thursday: black, soundless watermelons.
Friday: white watermelons.

Saturday: blue watermelons.

Sunday: brown watermelons.

Today would be a day of gray watermelons. I like best tomorrow: the black, soundless watermelon days. When you cut them they make no noise, and taste very sweet.

They are very good for making things that have no sound. I remember there was a man who used to make clocks from the black, soundless watermelons and his clocks were silent.

The man made six or seven of these clocks and then he died.

There is one of the clocks hanging over his grave. It is hanging from the branches of an apple tree and sways in the winds that go up and down the river. It of course does not keep time any more.

Pauline woke up while I was putting my shoes on.

"Hello," she said, rubbing her eyes. "You're up. I wonder what time it is."

"It's about six."

"I have to cook breakfast this morning at iDEATH," she said. "Come over here and give me a kiss and then tell me what you would like for breakfast."

Hands

WE WALKED BACK TO iDEATH, holding hands. Hands are very nice things, especially after they have travelled back from making love.

Margaret Again, Again

I SAT IN THE KITCHEN at iDEATH, watching Pauline make the batter for hot cakes, my favorite food. She put a lot of flour and eggs and good things into a great blue bowl and stirred the batter with a big wooden spoon, almost too large for her hand.

She was wearing a real nice dress and her hair was combed on top of her head and I had stopped and picked some flowers for her hair when we walked down the road.

They were bluebells.

"I wonder if Margaret will be here today," she said. "I'll be glad when we're talking again."

"Don't worry about it," I said. "Everything will be all right."

"It's just—well, Margaret and I have been such good friends. I'd always liked you before, but I never thought we'd ever be anything but friends.

"You and Margaret were so close for years. I just hope everything works out, and Margaret finds someone new and will be my friend again."

"Don't worry."

Fred came into the kitchen just to say, "Ummmm—hot cakes," and then left.

41

Strawberries

CHARLEY MUST HAVE EATEN a dozen hot cakes himself. I have never seen him eat so many hot cakes, and Fred ate a few more than Charley.

It was quite a sight.

There was also a big platter of bacon and lots of fresh milk and a big pot of strong coffee, and there was a bowl of fresh strawberries, too.

A girl came by from the town and left them off just before breakfast. She was a gentle girl.

Pauline said, "Thank you, and what a lovely dress you have on this morning. Did you make it yourself? You must have because it's so pretty."

"Oh, thank you," the girl said, blushing. "I just wanted to bring some strawberries to iDEATH for breakfast, so I got up very early and gathered them down by the river."

Pauline ate one of the berries and gave one of them to me. "They are such fine berries," Pauline said. "You must know a good place to get them, and you must show me where that place is."

"It's right near that statue of a rutabaga by the ball park, just down from where that funny green bridge is," the girl said. She was about fourteen years old and very pleased that her strawberries were a big hit at iDEATH.

All of the strawberries were eaten at breakfast, and again as for the hot cakes: "These are really wonderful hot cakes," Charley said.

"Would you like some more?" Pauline said.

"Maybe another one if there is any more batter."

"There's plenty," Pauline said. "How about you, Fred?"

"Well, maybe just one more."

The Schoolteacher

AFTER BREAKFAST I kissed Pauline while she was washing the dishes and went with Fred down to the Watermelon Works to see something he wanted to show me about the plank press.

We took a long leisurely stroll down there, through the morning of a gray sun. It looked like it might rain but of course it would not. The first rain of the year would not start until the 12th day of October.

"Margaret wasn't there this morning," Fred said.

"No, she wasn't," I said.

We stopped and talked to the schoolteacher who was taking his students for a walk in the woods. While we talked to him all the children sat down in the grass nearby, and were kind of gathered together like a ring of mushrooms or daisies.

"Well, how's the book coming?" the schoolteacher said.

"All right," I said.

"I'll be very curious to see it," the schoolteacher said. "You always had a way with words. I still remember that essay you wrote on weather when you were in the sixth grade. That was quite something.

"Your description of the winter clouds was very accurate and quite moving at the same time and contained a certain amount of poetic content. Yes, I am quite interested in reading your book. Will you give any hints on what it is about?"

Fred meanwhile looked very bored. He went and sat down with the children. He started talking to a boy about something.

"Have you expanded your essay on weather or is the book about something else?"

The boy was very interested in what Fred was saying. A couple of other kids moved closer.

"Oh, it's just coming along," I said. "It's pretty hard to talk about. But you'll be one of the first I'll show it to when it's done."

"I've always had faith in you as a writer," the schoolteacher said. "For a long time I thought about writing a book myself, but teaching absorbs just too much of my time."

Fred took something out of his pocket. He showed it to the boy. He looked at it and passed it on to the other children.

"Yes, I thought that I would write a book about teaching, but so far I've been too busy teaching to write. But it is very inspiring to me to have one of my former star pupils carry the glorious banner for what I myself have been too busy to do. Good luck."

"Thank you."

Fred put the thing back in his pocket and the schoolteacher got all of his students back on their feet, and off they went to the woods.

He was talking to them about something very important. I could tell because he pointed back at me, and then he pointed at a cloud that was drifting low overhead.

Under the Plank Press

As we neared the Watermelon Works the air was full of the sweet smell of the sugar being boiled in the vats. There were great layers and strips and shapes of sugar hardening out in the sun: red sugar, golden sugar, gray sugar, black, soundless sugar, white sugar, blue sugar, brown sugar.

"The sugar sure looks good," Fred said.

"Yeah."

I waved at Ed and Mike, whose job it is to keep the birds off the sugar. They waved back, and then one of them began chasing after a bird.

There are about a dozen people who work at the Watermelon Works, and we went inside. There were great fires going under the two vats, and Peter was feeding wood into them. He looked hot and sweaty, but that was his natural condition.

"How's the sugar coming?" I said.

"Fine," he said. "Lot of sugar. How are things at iDEATH?"

"Good," I said.

"What's this about you and Pauline?"

"Just gossip," I said.

I like Pete. We've been friends for years. When I was a child I used to come down to the Watermelon Works and help him feed the fires.

46

"I'll bet Margaret's mad," he said. "I hear she's really pining for you. That's what her brother says. She's just pining away."

"I don't know about that," I said.

"What are you down here for?" he said.

"I just came down here to chuck a piece of wood in the fire," I said. I reached over and picked up a large pine knot and put it in the fire under a vat.

"Just like old times," he said.

The foreman came out of his office and joined us. He looked kind of tired.

"Hi, Edgar," I said.

"Hello," he said. "How are you? Good morning, Fred."

"Good morning, boss."

"What brings you down here?" Edgar said.

"Fred wants to show me something."

"What's that, Fred?" Edgar said.

"It's a private thing, boss."

"Oh. Well, show away, then."

"Will do, boss."

"It's always good to see you down here," Edgar said to me.

"You look kind of tired," I said.

"Yeah, I stayed up late last night."

"Well, get some sleep tonight," I said.

"That's what I'm planning on. As soon as I get off work I'm going straight home to bed. Don't even think I'll eat any dinner, just grab a snack."

"Sleep's good for you," Fred said.

"I guess I'd better get back to the office," Edgar said. "I've got some paper work to do. See you later."

"Yeah, good-bye, Edgar."

The foreman went back to his office, and I went with Fred to the plank press. That's where we make watermelon planks. Today they were making golden planks.

Fred is the straw boss and the rest of his crew was already there, turning out planks.

47

"Good morning," the crew said.

"Good morning," Fred said. "Let's stop this thing here for a minute."

One of the crew turned off the switch and Fred had me come over very close and get down on my hands and knees and crawl under the press until we came to a very dark place and then he lit a match and showed me a bat hanging upside down from a housing.

"What do you think of that?" Fred said.

"Yeah," I said, staring at the bat.

"I found him there a couple of days ago. Doesn't that beat everything?" he said.

"It's got a head start," I said.

Until Lunch

AFTER HAVING ADMIRED Fred's bat and crawled out from underneath the plank press, I told him that I had to go up to my shack and do some work: plant some flowers and things.

"Are you going to have lunch at iDEATH?" he said.

"No, I think I'll just have a snack downtown at the cafe later on. Why don't you join me, Fred?"

"OK," he said. "I think they're serving frankfurters and sauerkraut today."

"That was yesterday," one of his crew volunteered.

"You're right," Fred said. "Today's meat loaf. How does that sound?"

"All right," I said. "I'll see you for lunch, then. About twelve."

I left Fred supervising the plank press with big golden planks of watermelon sugar coming down the chain. The Watermelon Works was bubbling and drying away, sweet and gentle in the warm gray sun.

And Ed and Mike were chasing after birds. Mike was running a robin off.

The Tombs

ON MY WAY to the shack, I decided to go down to the river where they were putting in a new tomb and look at the trout that always gather out of a great curiosity when the tombs are put in.

I passed through the town. It was kind of quiet with just a few people on the streets. I saw Doc Edwards going somewhere carrying his bag, and I waved at him.

He waved back and made a motion to show that he was on a very important errand. Somebody was probably sick in the town. I waved him on.

There were a couple of old people sitting in rocking chairs on the front porch of the hotel. One of them was rocking and the other one was asleep. The one that was asleep had a newspaper in his lap.

I could smell bread baking in the bakery and there were two horses tied up in front of the general store. I recognized one of the horses as being from iDEATH.

I walked out of the town and passed by some trees that were at the edge of a little watermelon patch. The trees had moss hanging from them.

A squirrel ran up into the branches of a tree. His tail was missing. I wondered what had happened to his tail. I guess he lost it someplace.

I sat down on a couch by the river. There was a statue of grass beside the couch. The blades were made from copper and had been turned to their natural color by the rain weight of years.

There were four or five guys putting in the tomb. They were the Tomb Crew. The tomb was being put into the bottom of the river. That's how we bury our dead here. Of course we used a lot less tombs when the tigers were in bloom.

But now we bury them all in glass coffins at the bottoms of rivers and put foxfire in the tombs, so they glow at night and we can appreciate what comes next.

I saw a bunch of trout gathered together to watch the tomb being put in. They were nice-looking rainbow trout. There were perhaps a hundred of them in a very small space in the river. The trout have a great curiosity about this activity, and many of them gather to watch.

The Tomb Crew had sunk the Shaft into the river and the pump was going away. They were doing the glass inlay work now. Soon the tomb would be complete and the door would be opened when it was needed and someone would go inside to stay there for the ages.

The Grand Old Trout

I SAW A TROUT that I have known for a long time watching the tomb being put in. It was The Grand Old Trout, raised as a fingerling in the trout hatchery at iDEATH. I knew this because he had the little iDEATH bell fastened to his jaw. He is many years old and weighs many pounds and moves slowly with wisdom.

The Grand Old Trout usually spends all of its time upstream by the Statue of Mirrors. I had spent many hours in the past watching this trout in the deep pool there. I guess he had been curious about this particular tomb and had come down to watch it being put in.

I wondered about this because The Grand Old Trout usually shows very little interest in watching the tombs being put in. I guess because he has seen so many before.

I remember once they were putting in a tomb just a little ways down from the Statue of Mirrors and he didn't move an inch in all the days that it took because it was such a hard tomb to put in.

The tomb collapsed just before completion. Charley came down and shook his head sadly, and the tomb had to be done all over again.

But now the trout was watching very intently this tomb being put in. He was hovering just a few inches above the bottom and ten feet away from the Shaft.

I went down and crouched by the river. The trout were not scared at all by the closeness of my appearance. The Grand Old Trout looked over at me.

I believe he recognized me, for he stared at me for a couple of minutes, and then he turned back to watching the tomb being put in, the final inlay work being done.

I stayed there for a little while by the river and when I left to go to my shack, The Grand Old Trout turned and stared at me. He was still staring at me when I was gone from sight, I thought.

Book Two:
inBOIL

Nine Things

IT WAS GOOD to be back at my shack, but there was a note on the door from Margaret. I read the note and it did not please me and I threw it away, so not even time could find it.

I sat down at my table and looked out the window, down to iDEATH. I had a few things to do with pen and ink and did them rapidly and without mistake, and put them away written in watermelonseed ink upon these sheets of sweet smelling wood made by Bill down at the shingle factory.

Then I thought that I would plant some flowers out by the potato statue, a bunch of them in a circle around that seven-foot potato would look nice.

I went and got some seeds from the chest that I keep my things in and noticed that everything was ajar, and so before planting the seeds, I put everything back in order.

I have nine things, more or less: a child's ball (I can't remember which child), a present given me nine years ago by Fred, my essay on weather, some numbers (1-24), an extra pair of overalls, a piece of blue metal, something from the Forgotten Works, a lock of hair that needs washing.

I kept the seeds out because I was going to put them in the ground around the potato. I have a few other things that I keep in my room at iDEATH. I have a nice room there off toward the trout hatchery.

I went outside and planted the seeds around the potato and wondered again who liked vegetables so much, and where were they buried, under what river or had a tiger eaten them a long time ago when the tiger's beautiful voice had said, "I like your statues very much, especially that rutabaga by the ball park, but alas. . ."

Margaret Again, Again, Again

I SPENT A HALF AN HOUR or so pacing back and forth on the bridge, but I did not once find that board that Margaret always steps on, that board she could not miss if all the bridges in the world were put together, formed into one single bridge, she'd step on that board.

A Nap

SUDDENLY I FELT very tired and decided to take a nap before lunch and went into the shack and lay down in my bed. I looked up at the ceiling, at the beams of watermelon sugar. I stared at the grain and was soon fast asleep.

I had a couple of small dreams. One of them was about a moth. The moth was balanced on an apple.

Then I had a long dream, which was again the history of inBOIL and that gang of his and the terrible things that happened just a few short months ago.

Whiskey

INBOIL and that gang of his lived in a little bunch of lousy shacks with leaky roofs near the Forgotten Works. They lived there until they were dead. I think there were about twenty of them. All men, like inBOIL, that were no good.

First there was just inBOIL who lived there. He got in a big fight one night with Charley and told him to go to hell and said he would sooner live by the Forgotten Works than in iDEATH.

"To hell with iDEATH," he said, and went and built himself a lousy shack by the Forgotten Works. He spent his time digging around in there and making whiskey from things.

Then a couple of other men went and joined up with him and from time to time, every once in a while, a new man would join them. You could always tell who they would be.

Before they joined inBOIL's gang, they would always be unhappy and nervous and shifty or have "light fingers" and talk a lot about things that good people did not understand nor wanted to.

They would grow more and more nervous and no account and then finally you would hear about them having joined inBOIL's gang and now they were working with him in the Forgotten Works, and being paid in whiskey that inBOIL made from forgotten things.

61

Whiskey Again

INBOIL was about fifty years old, I guess, and was born and raised at iDEATH. I remember sitting upon his knee as a child and having him tell me stories. He knew some pretty good ones, too . . . and Margaret was there.

Then he turned bad. It happened over a couple of years. He kept getting mad at things that were of no importance and going off by himself to the trout hatchery at iDEATH.

He began spending a lot of time at the Forgotten Works, and Charley would ask him what he was doing and INBOIL would say, "Oh, nothing. Just off by myself."

"What kind of things do you find when you're digging down there?"

"Oh, nothing," INBOIL lied.

He became very removed from people and then his speech would be strange, slurred and his movements became jerky and his temper bad, and he spent a lot of time at night in the trout hatchery and sometimes he would laugh out loud and you could hear this enormous laugh that had now become his, echoing through the rooms and halls, and into the very changing of iDEATH: the indescribable way it changes that we like so much, that suits us.

The Big Fight

THE BIG FIGHT between inBOIL and Charley occurred at dinner one night. Fred was passing some mashed potatoes to me when it happened.

The fight had been building up for weeks. inBOIL's laughter had grown louder and louder until it was almost impossible to sleep at night.

inBOIL was drunk all the time, and he would listen to no one about anything, not even Charley. He wouldn't even listen to Charley. He told Charley to mind his own business. "Mind your own business."

One afternoon Pauline, who was just a child, found him passed out in the bathtub, singing dirty songs. She was frightened and he had a bottle of that stuff he brewed down at the Forgotten Works. He smelled horrible and it took three men to lift him out of the bathtub and get him to bed.

"Here are the mashed potatoes," Fred said.

I was just putting a big scoop of them on my plate to soak up the rest of the gravy when inBOIL, who had not touched a single bite of his fried chicken and it was growing cold in front of him, turned to Charley and said, "Do you know what's wrong with this place?"

"No, what's wrong, inBOIL? You seem to have all the answers these days. Tell me."

63

"I *will* tell you. This place stinks. This isn't iDEATH at all. This is just a figment of your imagination. All of you guys here are just a bunch of clucks, doing clucky things at your clucky iDEATH.

"iDEATH—ha, don't make me laugh. This place is nothing but a claptrap. You wouldn't know iDEATH if it walked up and bit you.

"I know more about iDEATH than all of you guys, especially Charley here who thinks he's something extra. I know more about iDEATH in my little finger than all you guys know put together.

"You haven't the slightest idea what's going on here. I know. I know. I know. To hell with your iDEATH. I've forgotten more iDEATH than you guys will ever know. I'm going down to the Forgotten Works to live. You guys can have this damn rat hole."

inBOIL got up and threw his fried chicken on the floor and stomped out of the place, travelling very unevenly. There was stunned silence at the table and no one could say anything for a long time.

Then Fred said, "Don't feel bad about it, Charley. He'll be sober tomorrow and everything will be different. He's just drunk again and as soon as he sobers up, he'll be better."

"No, I think he's gone for good," Charley said. "I hope it all works out for the best."

Charley looked very sad and we were all sad, too, because inBOIL was Charley's brother. We all sat there looking at our food.

Time

THE YEARS PASSED with inBOIL living down by the Forgotten Works and gathering slowly a gang of men who were just like him, believed in the things he did, and acted his way and went digging in the Forgotten Works and drank whiskey brewed from the things they found.

Sometimes they would sober up one of the gang and send him into town to sell forgotten things that were particularly beautiful or curious or books which we used for fuel then because there were millions of them lying around in the Forgotten Works.

They would get bread and food and whatnot for the forgotten things and so lived without having to do anything besides dig and drink.

Margaret grew up to be a very pretty young woman and we went steady together. Margaret came over to my shack one day.

I could tell it was her even before she was there because I heard her step on that board she always steps on, and it pleased me and made my stomach tingle like a bell set ajar.

She knocked on the door.

"Come in, Margaret," I said.

She came in and kissed me. "What are you doing today?" she said.

"I have to go down to iDEATH and work on my statue."

"Are you still working on that bell?" she said.

"Yes," I said. "It's coming along rather slowly. It's taking too long. I'll be glad when it's done. I'm tired of the thing."

"What are you going to do afterwards?" she said.

"I don't know. Is there anything you want to do, honey?"

"Yes," she said. "I want to go down to the Forgotten Works and poke around."

"Again?" I said. "You certainly like to spend a lot of time down there."

"It's a curious place," she said.

"You're about the only woman who likes that place. inBOIL and that gang of his put the other women off."

"I like it down there. inBOIL is harmless. All he wants to do is stay drunk."

"All right," I said. "It's nothing, honey. Meet me down at iDEATH later on. I'll be with you as soon as I put in a few more hours on that bell."

"Are you going down now?" she said.

"No, I have a few things I want to do here first."

"Can I help?" she said.

"No, they're just a few things I have to do alone."

"OK, then. I'll see you."

"Give me a kiss first," I said.

She came over and I held her in my arms very close and kissed Margaret upon the mouth, and then she went off laughing.

The Bell

AFTER WHILE I went down to iDEATH and worked on that bell. It was not coming at all and finally I was just sitting there on a chair, staring at it.

My chisel was hanging limply in my hand, and then I put it down on the table and absentmindedly covered it up with a rag.

Fred came in and saw me sitting there staring at the bell. He left without saying anything. It hardly even looked like a bell.

Finally Margaret came and rescued me. She was wearing a blue dress and had a ribbon in her hair and carried a basket to put things in that she found at the Forgotten Works.

"How's it coming?" she said.

"It's finished," I said.

"It doesn't look finished," she said.

"It's finished," I said.

Pauline

WE SAW Charley as we were leaving iDEATH. He was sitting on his favorite couch by the river, feeding little pieces of bread to some trout that had gathered there.

"Where you kids going?" he said.

"Oh, just out for a walk," Margaret said, before I could say anything.

"Well, have a good walk," he said. "Lovely day, isn't it? Great big beautiful blue sun shining away."

"It sure is," I said.

Pauline came into the room and walked over and joined us. "Hello, there," she said.

"Hi."

"What do you want for dinner, Charley?" she said.

"Roast beef," Charley said, joking.

"Well, that's what you'll have then."

"What a nice surprise," Charley said. "Is it my birthday?"

"No. How are you people?"

"We're fine," I said.

"We're going for a walk," Margaret said.

"That sounds like fun. See you later."

The Forgotten Works

NOBODY KNOWS how old the Forgotten Works are, reaching as they do into distances that we cannot travel nor want to.

Nobody has been very far into the Forgotten Works, except that guy Charley said who wrote a book about them, and I wonder what his trouble was, to spend weeks in there.

The Forgotten Works just go on and on and on and on and on and on and on and on. You get the picture. It's a big place, much bigger than we are.

Margaret and I went down there, holding hands for we were going steady, through the sun of a blue day and white luminous clouds drifting overhead.

We crossed over many rivers and walked by many things, and then we could see the sun reflecting off the roofs at inBOIL's bunch of leaky shacks which were at the entrance to the Forgotten Works.

There is a gate right there. Beside the gate is the statue of a forgotten thing. There is a sign above the gate that says:

THIS IS THE ENTRANCE TO THE FORGOTTEN WORKS
BE CAREFUL
YOU MIGHT GET LOST

A Conversation with Trash

INBOIL came out to greet us. His clothes were all wrinkled and dirty and so was he. He looked like a mess and he was drunk. "Hello," he said. "Down here again, huh?" he said, more to Margaret than to me, though he looked at me when he said it. That's the kind of person INBOIL is.

"Just visiting," I said.

He laughed at that. A couple of other guys came out of shacks and stared at us. They all looked like INBOIL. They had made the same mess out of themselves by being evil and drinking that whiskey made from forgotten things.

One of them, a yellow-haired one, sat down on a pile of disgusting objects and just stared at us like he was an animal.

"Good afternoon, INBOIL," Margaret said.

"Same to you, pretty."

Some of INBOIL's trash laughed at that and I looked at them hard and they shut up. One of them wiped his hand across his mouth and went inside his shack.

"Just being social," INBOIL said. "Don't take no offense."

"We're just down here to look at the Forgotten Works," I said.

"Well, she's all yours," INBOIL said, pointing at the Forgotten Works that gradually towered above us until the big piles of forgotten things were mountains that went on for at least a million miles.

70

In There

YOU MIGHT GET LOST
and we walked through the gate into the Forgotten Works.
Margaret started poking around for things that she might like.
There were no plants growing and no animals living in the
Forgotten Works. There was not even so much as a blade of
grass in there, and the birds refused to fly over the place.

I sat down on something that looked like a wheel and watched
Margaret take a forgotten sticklike thing and poke around a
small pile of stuffed things.

I saw something lying at my feet. It was a piece of ice frozen
into the shape of a thumb, but the thumb had a hump on it.

It was a hunchback thumb and very cold but started to melt
in my hand.

The fingernail melted away and then I dropped the thing and
it lay at my feet, not melting any more, though the air was not
cold and the sun was hot and blue in the sky.

"Have you found anything you like?" I said.

The Master of the Forgotten Works

INBOIL came in and joined us. It did not overly please me to see him. He had a bottle of whiskey with him. His nose was red.

"Find anything you like?" INBOIL said.

"Not yet," Margaret said.

I gave INBOIL a dirty look but it rolled off him like water off a duck's back.

"I found some real good interesting things today," INBOIL said. "Just before I went to have lunch."

Lunch!

"They're about a quarter-of-a-mile in. I can show you the place," INBOIL said.

Before I could say no, Margaret said yes, and I was not happy about it, but she had already committed herself and I did not want to make a scene with her in front of INBOIL, so he would have something to tell his gang and they would all laugh.

That wouldn't make me feel good at all.

So we followed that drunken bum in what he said was only a quarter-of-a-mile, but it seemed like a mile to me, weaving in and out, climbing higher and higher into the Piles.

"Nice day, isn't it?" INBOIL said, stopping to catch his breath by a large pile of what looked like cans, maybe.

"Yes, it is," Margaret said, smiling at INBOIL and pointing out a cloud that she particularly liked.

72

That really disgusted me: a decent woman smiling at inBOIL. I could not help but wonder, what next?

Finally we arrived at that pile of stuff inBOIL thought was so great and had taken us so far into the Forgotten Works to see.

"Why, they're beautiful," Margaret said, smiling and went over and began putting them into her basket, the basket she had brought for such things.

I looked at them but they didn't show me anything. They were kind of ugly, if you want the truth. inBOIL leaned up against a forgotten thing that was just his size.

The Way Back

MARGARET AND I had a very long and quiet walk back to iDEATH.
I did not volunteer to carry her basket for her.

It was heavy and she was hot and sweaty and we had to stop
many times for her to rest.

We were sitting on a bridge. The bridge was made from
stones gathered at a distance and placed in their proper order.

"What's wrong?" she said. "What have I done?"

"Nothing's wrong. You've done nothing."

"Then why are you mad at me?"

"I'm not mad at you."

"Yes, you are."

"No, I'm not."

Something Is Going to Happen

THE NEXT MONTH it happened and no one knew what was coming. How could we imagine such a thing was going on in inBOIL's mind?

It had taken years to get over the tigers and the terrible things they had done to us. Why would anyone want to do something else? I don't know.

During the weeks before it happened everything went on as normal at iDEATH. I started working on another statue and Margaret kept going down to the Forgotten Works.

The statue did not go well and pretty soon I was only going down to iDEATH and staring at the statue. It just wasn't coming along which was nothing new for me. I had never had much luck at statues. I was thinking about getting a job down at the Watermelon Works.

Sometimes Margaret went down to the Forgotten Works by herself. It worried me. She was so pretty and inBOIL and that gang of his were so ugly. They might get ideas.

Why did she want to go down there all the time?

Rumors

TOWARD THE END of the month strange rumors began coming up from the Forgotten Works, rumors of violent denouncements of iDEATH by inBOIL.

There were rumors about him ranting and raving that iDEATH was all wrong the way we did it, and he knew how it should be done and then he said we handled the trout hatchery all wrong. It was a disgrace.

Imagine inBOIL saying anything about us, and there was a rumor about us being sissies and then something about the tigers that no one could understand.

Something about the tigers being a good deal.

I went down to the Forgotten Works with Margaret one afternoon. I didn't want to go down there, but I didn't want her to go down there alone either.

She wanted to get more things for her forgotten collection. She already had more things than were necessary.

She had filled her shack up and her room at iDEATH with these things. She even wanted to store some of them in my shack. I said NO.

I asked inBOIL what was up. He was drunk as usual, and his gang of bums was gathered around.

"You guys don't know anything about iDEATH. I'm going to

76

show you something about it soon. What real iDEATH is like," inBOIL said.

"You guys are a bunch of sissies. Only the tigers had any guts. I'm going to show you. We're going to show you all." He addressed this last thing to his gang. They cheered and held their bottles of whiskey up high, reaching toward the red sun.

The Way Back Again

"WHY DO YOU go down there?" I said.

"I just like forgotten things. I'm collecting them. I want a collection of them. I think they're cute. What's wrong with that?"

"What do you mean, what's wrong with that? Didn't you hear what that drunken bum said about us?"

"What does that have to do with forgotten things?" she said.

"They drink the stuff," I said.

Dinner That Night

DINNER THAT NIGHT was troubled at iDEATH. Everybody played with their food. Al had cooked up a mess of carrots. They were good, mixed with honey and spices, but nobody cared.

Everybody was worried about inBOIL. Pauline didn't touch her food. Neither did Charley. Strange thing, though: Margaret ate like a horse.

There had been a longish period of silence when Charley finally said, "I don't know what's going to happen. It looks serious. I've been afraid something like this was going to happen for a long time, ever since inBOIL got involved with the Forgotten Works, and took to making that whiskey of his, and getting men to go down there and live his kind of life.

"I've known something was going to happen. It's been due for a long time, and now it looks like it's here or will be shortly. Perhaps tomorrow. Who knows?"

"What are we going to do?" Pauline said. "What can we do?"

"Just wait," Charley said. "That's about all. We can't threaten them or defend ourselves until they've done something, and who knows what they are going to do. They won't tell us.

"I went down there myself yesterday morning, and I asked inBOIL what was up and he said, we'd see soon enough. They'd show us what iDEATH really was, none of the false stuff we have.

79

What do you know about this, Margaret? You've spent a lot of time down there lately."

Everybody looked at her.

"I don't know anything. I just get forgotten things down there. They don't tell me anything. They're always very nice to me."

Everybody tried hard not to look away from Margaret, but they couldn't help themselves, and looked away.

"We can take care of anything that happens," Fred said, breaking the silence. "Those drunken bums can't do anything we can't handle."

"You bet," Old Chuck said, though he was very old.

"You're right," Pauline said. "We can handle them. We live at iDEATH."

Margaret went right back to eating her carrots as if nothing had happened.

Pauline Again

I WAS VERY ANGRY with Margaret. She wanted to sleep with me at iDEATH, but I said, "NO, I want to go up to my shack and be alone."

She was very hurt by this and went off to the trout hatchery. I didn't care. Her performance at dinner had really disgusted me.

On my way out of iDEATH, I met Pauline in the living room. She was carrying a painting that she was going to put up on the wall.

"Hello," I said. "That's a lovely painting you have there. Did you paint that yourself?"

"Yes, I did."

"It looks very good."

The painting was of iDEATH a long time ago during one of its many changes. The painting looked like iDEATH used to look.

"I didn't know you painted," I said.

"Just in my spare time."

"It's really a nice painting."

"Thank you."

Pauline kind of blushed. I had never seen her blush before or perhaps I had not remembered so. It became her.

"You think everything is going to be all right, don't you?" she said, changing the subject.

"Yes," I said. "Don't worry."

Faces

I LEFT iDEATH and started up the road to my shack. It was suddenly a very cold night and the stars shone like ice. I wished I had brought my Mackinaw. I walked up the road until I saw the lanterns on the bridges.

They were the lanterns of a beautiful child and a trout on the real bridge, and the tiger lanterns on the abandoned bridge.

I could barely see the statue of somebody who had been killed by the tigers, but nobody knows who it was. So many were killed by the tigers until we killed the last tiger and burned its body at iDEATH and built the trout hatchery right over the spot.

The statue was standing in the river by the bridges. It looked sad as if it did not want to be a statue of somebody killed by the tigers a long time ago.

I stopped and stared at a distance. A little while passed and then I went to the bridge. I crossed through the dark tunnel of the covered real bridge, past the glowing faces, and up into the piney woods toward my shack.

Shack

I STOPPED ON THE BRIDGE to my shack. It felt good under my feet, made from all the things that I like, the things that suit me. I stared at my mother. She was only another shadow now against the night, but once she had been a good woman.

I went inside the shack and lit my lantern with a six-inch match. The watermelontrout oil burned with a beautiful light. It is a fine oil.

We mix watermelon sugar and trout juice and special herbs all together and in their proper time to make this fine oil that we use to light our world.

I was very sleepy but I didn't feel like sleeping. The sleepier I got, the less I felt like sleeping. I lay on my bed for a long time without taking off my clothes, and I left the lantern on and stared at the shadows in the room.

They were rather nice shadows for a time that was so ominous, that drew so near and all enclosing. I was so sleepy now that my eyes refused to close. The lids would not budge down. They were statues of eyes.

The Girl with the Lantern

AT LAST I couldn't stand lying there in bed any longer without sleeping. I went for one of my walks at night. I put on my red Mackinaw, so I wouldn't be cold. I guess it is this trouble that I have with sleeping that causes me to walk.

I went walking down by the aqueduct. That's a good place to walk. The aqueduct is about five miles long, but we don't know why because there is already water every place. There must be two or three hundred rivers here.

Charley himself hasn't the slightest idea why they built the aqueduct. "Maybe they were short of water a long time ago, and that's why they built the thing. I don't know. Don't ask me."

I once had a dream about the aqueduct being a musical instrument filled with water and bells hanging by small watermelon chains right at the top of the water and the water making the bells ring.

I told the dream to Fred and he said that it sounded all right to him. "That would really make beautiful music," he said.

I walked along the aqueduct for a while and then just stood there motionless for a long time where the aqueduct crosses the river by the Statue of Mirrors. I could see the light coming from all the tombs in the river down there. It's a favorite spot to be buried.

I climbed up a ladder on one of the columns and sat on the edge of the aqueduct, up about twenty feet, with my legs dangling over the edge.

I sat there for a long time without thinking about anything or noticing anything any more. I didn't want to. The night was passing with me sitting on the aqueduct.

Then I saw a lantern faraway and moving out of the piney woods. The lantern came down a road and then crossed over bridges and went through watermelon patches and stopped sometimes by the road, first this road and then that road.

I knew who the lantern belonged to. It was in the hand of a girl. I had seen her many times before walking at night, over the years.

But I had never seen the girl up close and I didn't know who she was. I knew she was sort of like me. Sometimes she had trouble sleeping at night.

It always comforted me when I saw her out there. I had never tried to find out who she was by going after her or even telling anyone about seeing her at night.

She was in a strange way mine and it comforted me to see her. I thought she was very pretty, but I didn't know what color hair she had.

Chickens

THE GIRL WITH THE LANTERN had left hours ago. I climbed down
from the aqueduct and stretched my legs. I walked back to
iDEATH in the dawn of a golden sun which would bring I knew
not what from inBOIL and that gang of his. We could only wait
and see.

The countryside was beginning to stir. I saw a farmer going
out to milk his cows. He waved when he saw me. He had on a
funny hat.

The roosters were beginning to crow. Their beak trumpets
travelled a loud and great distance. I arrived at iDEATH just before sunrise.

There were a couple of white chickens that had escaped from
a farmer someplace out in front of iDEATH pecking at the ground.
They looked at me and then they flew away. They were freshly
escaped. You could tell because their wings did not work like
real birds.

Bacon

AFTER A GOOD BREAKFAST of hot cakes and scrambled eggs and bacon, inBOIL and that gang of his arrived drunk at iDEATH, and it all began, then.

"This is really a good breakfast," Fred said to Pauline.

"Thank you."

Margaret was not there. I don't know where she was at. Pauline was there, though. She looked good, wearing a pretty dress.

Then we heard the front door bell ring. Old Chuck said he heard voices but it was impossible to hear voices from that distance.

"I'll get the door," Al said. He got up and left the kitchen and walked through the hall that led under the river to the living room.

"I wonder who it is," Charley said. I think Charley already knew who it was because he put down his fork and pushed his plate away.

Breakfast was over.

Al came back a few minutes later. He looked strange and worried. "It's inBOIL," he said. "He wants to see you, Charley. He wants to see all of us."

Now we all looked strange and worried.

We got up and went through the hall under the river and came out in the living room, right beside Pauline's painting. We went out on the front porch of iDEATH and there was inBOIL waiting, drunk.

Prelude

"YOU PEOPLE THINK you know about iDEATH. You don't know anything about iDEATH. You don't know anything about iDEATH," inBOIL said, and then there was wild laughter from that gang of his, who were just as drunk as he.

"Not a damn thing. You're all at a masquerade party," and then there was wild laughter from that gang of his.

"We're going to show you what iDEATH is really about," and then there was wild laughter.

"What do you know that we don't know?" Charley said.

"Let us show you. Let us into the trout hatchery and we'll show you a thing or two. Are you afraid to find out about iDEATH? What it really means? What a mockery you've made of it? All of you. And you, Charley, more than the rest of these clowns."

"Come, then," Charley said. "Show us iDEATH."

An Exchange

INBOIL and that gang of his staggered into iDEATH. "What a dump," one of them said. Their eyes were all red from that stuff they made and drank in such large quantities.

We crossed the metal bridge over the little river in the living room and went down the hall that leads to the trout hatchery.

One of INBOIL's gang was so drunk that he fell down and the others picked him up. They almost had to carry him along because he was so drunk. He kept saying over and over again, "When are we going to get to iDEATH?"

"You are at iDEATH."

"What is this?"

"iDEATH."

"Oh. When are we going to get to iDEATH?"

Margaret was nowhere around. I walked beside Pauline to kind of shield her from INBOIL and his trash. INBOIL saw her and came over. His overalls looked as if they had never been washed.

"Hi, Pauline," he said. "How are tricks?"

"You disgusting man," she replied.

INBOIL laughed.

"I'll mop the floor after you leave here," she said. "Wherever you walk is filth."

"Don't be that way," INBOIL said.

90

"How should I be?" Pauline said. "Look at you."

I had gone over to shield Pauline from inBOIL and now I almost had to step between them. Pauline was very mad. I had never seen Pauline mad before. She had quite a temper.

inBOIL laughed again and then he broke away from her and went up and joined Charley. Charley was not happy to see him either.

It was a strange procession travelling down the hall. "When are we going to get to iDEATH?"

The Trout Hatchery

THE TROUT HATCHERY at iDEATH was built years ago when the last tiger was killed and burned on the spot. We built the trout hatchery right there. The walls went up around the ashes.

The hatchery is small but designed with great care. The trays and ponds are made from watermelon sugar and stones gathered at a great distance and placed there in the order of that distance.

The water for the hatchery comes from the little river that joins up later with the main river in the living room. The sugar used is golden and blue.

There are two people buried at the bottom of the ponds in the hatchery. You look down past the young trout and see them lying there in their coffins, staring from beyond the glass doors. They wanted it that way, so they got it, being as they were keepers of the hatchery and at the same time, Charley's folks.

The hatchery has a beautiful tile floor with the tiles put together so gracefully that it's almost like music. It's a swell place to dance.

There is a statue of the last tiger in the hatchery. The tiger is on fire in the statue. We are all watching it.

inBOIL's iDEATH

"ALL RIGHT," Charley said. "Tell us about iDEATH. We're curious now about what you've been saying for years about us not knowing about iDEATH, about you knowing all the answers. Let's hear some of those answers."

"OK," inBOIL said. "This is what it's all about. You don't know what's really going on with iDEATH. The tigers knew more about iDEATH than you know. You killed all the tigers and burned the last one in here.

"That was all wrong. The tigers should never have been killed. The tigers were the true meaning of iDEATH. Without the tigers there could be no iDEATH, and you killed the tigers and so iDEATH went away, and you've lived here like a bunch of clucks ever since. I'm going to bring back iDEATH. We're all going to bring back iDEATH. My gang here and me. I've been thinking about it for years and now we're going to do it. iDEATH will be again."

inBOIL reached into his pocket and took out a jackknife.

"What are you going to do with that knife?" Charley said.

"I'll show you," inBOIL said. He pulled the blade out. It looked sharp. "This is iDEATH," he said, and took the knife and cut off his thumb and dropped it into a tray filled with trout just barely hatched. The blood started running down his hand and dripping on the floor.

93

Then all of inBOIL's gang took out jackknives and cut off their thumbs and dropped their thumbs here and there, in this tray, that pond until there were thumbs and blood all over the place.

The one who didn't know where he was said, "When do I cut off my thumb?"

"Right now," somebody said.

So he cut off his thumb, unevenly because he was so drunk. He did it in such a way that there was still part of the fingernail fastened to his hand.

"Why have you done this?" Charley said.

"It's only a beginning," inBOIL said. "This is what iDEATH should really look like."

"You all look silly," Charley said. "Without your thumbs."

"It's only a beginning," inBOIL said. "All right, men. Let's cut off our noses."

"Hail, iDEATH," they all shouted and cut off their noses. The one who was so drunk also put out his eye. They took their noses and dropped them all over the place.

One of them put his nose in Fred's hand. Fred took the nose and threw it in the guy's face.

Pauline did not act like a woman should under these circumstances. She was not afraid or made ill by this at all. She just kept getting madder and madder and madder. Her face was red with anger.

"All right, men. Off with your ears."

"Hail, iDEATH," and then there were ears all over the place and the trout hatchery was drowning in blood.

The one who was so drunk forgot that he had cut his right ear off already and was trying to cut it off again and was very confused because the ear wasn't there.

"Where's my ear?" he said. "I can't cut it off."

By now inBOIL and all his gang were bleeding to death. Some of them were already beginning to grow weak from the loss of blood and were sitting down on the floor.

inBOIL was STILL up and cutting fingers off his hands. "This is iDEATH," he said. "Oh, boy. This is really iDEATH." Finally he had to sit down, too, so he could bleed to death.

They were all on the floor now.

"I hope you think you've proved something," Charley said. "I don't think you've proved anything."

"We've proved iDEATH," inBOIL said.

Pauline suddenly started to leave the room. I went over to her, almost slipping on the blood and falling down.

"Are you all right?" I said, not knowing quite what to say. "Can I help you?"

"No," she said, on her way out. "I'm going to go get a mop and clean this mess up." When she said mess, she looked directly at inBOIL.

She left the hatchery and came back shortly with a mop. They were almost all dead now, except for inBOIL. He was still talking about iDEATH. "See, we've done it," he said.

Pauline started mopping up the blood and wringing it out into a bucket. When the bucket was almost full of blood, inBOIL died. "I am iDEATH," he said.

"You're an asshole," Pauline said.

And the last thing that inBOIL ever saw was Pauline standing beside him, wringing his blood out of the mop into the bucket.

Wheelbarrow

"WELL, that's that," Charley said.

inBOIL's sightless eyes stared at the statue of the tiger. There were many sightless eyes staring in the hatchery.

"Yeah," Fred said. "I wonder what it was all about."

"I don't know," Charley said. "I think they shouldn't have drunk that whiskey made from forgotten things. It was a mistake."

"Yeah."

We all joined Pauline in cleaning up the place, mopping up the blood and carting the bodies away. We used a wheelbarrow.

A Parade

"HERE, help me get this wheelbarrow down the stairs."

"There."

"Ah, thank you."

We piled the bodies out in front. No one knew quite what to do with them, except that we didn't want them in iDEATH any more.

A lot of people from the town had come up to see what was going on. There were maybe a hundred people there by the time we got the last body wheeled out.

"What happened?" the schoolteacher said.

"They made a mess out of themselves," Old Chuck said.

"Where are their thumbs and features?" Doc Edwards asked.

"Right over there in that bucket," Old Chuck said. "They cut them off with their jackknives. We don't know why."

"What are we going to do with the bodies?" Fred said. "We're not going to put them in tombs, are we?"

"No," Charley said. "We have to do something else."

"Take them to their shacks at the Forgotten Works," Pauline said. "Burn them. Burn their shacks. Burn them together and then forget them."

"That's a good idea," Charley said. "Let's get some wagons and take them down there. What a terrible thing."

We put the bodies in the wagons. By then almost everybody in watermelon sugar had gathered at iDEATH. We all started down to the Forgotten Works together.

We started off very slowly. We looked like a parade barely moving toward YOU MIGHT GET LOST. I walked beside Pauline.

Bluebells

THERE WAS a warm golden sun shining down on us and on the slowly nearing Piles of the Forgotten Works. We crossed rivers and bridges and walked beside farms, meadows and through the piney woods and by fields of watermelons.

The piles of the Forgotten works were like chunks of half-mountains and half-apparatus that glowed like gold.

An almost festive spirit was coming now from the crowd. They were relieved that inBOIL and that gang of his were dead.

Children began picking flowers along the way and pretty soon there were many flowers in the parade, so that it became a kind of vase filled with roses and daffodils and poppies and bluebells.

"It's over," Pauline said, and then, turning, she threw her arms around me and gave me a very friendly hug to prove that it was all over. I felt her body against me.

Margaret Again, Again, Again, Again

INBOIL and the bodies of his gang were put into a shack and drenched with watermelontrout oil. We brought along a barrelful for that purpose and then all the other shacks were drenched with watermelontrout oil.

All the people stood back and just as Charley was getting ready to set fire to the shack where the bodies were, Margaret came waltzing out of the Forgotten Works.

"What's up?" she said. She acted as if nothing had happened, as if we were all down there on some kind of picnic.

"Where have you been?" Charley said, looking a little bewildered at Margaret, who was as cool as a cucumber.

"In the Forgotten Works," she said. "I came down here early this morning, before sunrise, to look for things. What's wrong? Why are you all down here at the Forgotten Works?"

"Don't you know what happened?" Charley said.

"No," she said.

"Did you see INBOIL when you came down here this morning?"

"No," she said. "They were all asleep. What's wrong?" She looked all around. "Where's INBOIL?"

"I don't even know if I can tell you," Charley said. "He's dead and all his gang, too."

"Dead. You must be joking."

"Why? No, they came up to iDEATH a couple of hours ago and they all killed themselves in the trout hatchery. We've brought their bodies down here to burn them. They made a terrible scene."

"I don't believe it," Margaret said. "I just can't believe it. What kind of joke is this?"

"It's no joke," Charley said.

Margaret looked around. She could see that almost everybody was there. She saw me standing beside Pauline and she ran over to me and said, "Is it true?"

"Yes."

"Why?"

"I don't know. None of us do. They just came up to iDEATH and killed themselves. It's a mystery to us."

"Oh no," Margaret said. "How did they do it?"

"With jackknives."

"Oh, no," Margaret said. She was very shocked, dazed. She grabbed ahold of my hand.

"This morning?" she said, almost to no one now.

"Yes."

Her hand felt cold and awkward in my hand as if the fingers were too small to fit. I could only stare at her who had disappeared into the Forgotten Works that morning.

Shack Fever

CHARLEY TOOK a six-inch match and set fire to the shack that contained inBOIL and the bodies of his gang. We all stood back and the flames went up higher and higher and burned with that beautiful light that watermelontrout oil makes.

Then Charley set fire to the other shacks and they burned just as brightly, and pretty soon the heat was so bad that we had to stand farther and farther back until we were in the fields.

We watched for an hour or so and the shacks were fairly gone by then. Charley stood there watching very quietly. inBOIL had once been his brother.

Some of the children were playing in the fields. They got tired of watching the fire. It had been very exciting at first, but then the children grew tired of it and decided to do something else.

Pauline sat down on the grass. The flames brought total peace to her face. She looked as if she had just been born.

I stopped holding Margaret's hand and she was still in a daze over what was happening. She sat by herself in the grass, holding her hands together as if they were dead.

As the flames diminished to very little, a strong wind came out of the Forgotten Works and scattered ashes rapidly through the air. After while Fred yawned, I dreamt.

Book Three:
Margaret

Job

I WOKE UP feeling refreshed and stared at my watermelon ceiling, how nice it looked, before getting out of bed. I wondered what time it was. I was supposed to meet Fred for lunch at the cafe in town.

I got up and went outside and stretched again on the front porch of my shack, feeling the cool stones under my bare feet, feeling their distance. I looked at the gray sun.

The river shone not quite lunch time yet, so I went over to the river and got some water and threw it in my face to finish the job of waking up.

Meat Loaf

I MET Fred at the cafe. He was already there, waiting for me. Doc Edwards was with him. Fred was looking at the menu.

"Hello," I said.

"Hi."

"Hello," Doc Edwards said.

"You were really in a hurry this morning," I said. "You looked like you needed a horse."

"That's right. I had to go deliver a baby. A litle girl joined us this morning."

"That's fine," I said. "Who's the lucky father?"

"Do you know Ron?"

"Yeah. He lives in that shack by the shoeshop. Right?"

"Yeah. That's Ron. He's got a fine little girl."

"You were really moving along. I didn't know you had that much speed left in you."

"Yes. Yes."

"How are you, Fred?" I said.

"Fine. I put in a good morning's work. What did you do?"

"Planted a few flowers."

"Did you work on your book?"

"No, I planted a few flowers and took a long nap."

"Lazyhead."

"By the way," Doc Edwards said. "How's that book coming along?"

"Oh, it's coming along."

"Fine. What's it about?"

"Just what I'm writing down: one word after another."

"Good."

The waitress came over and asked us what we were having for lunch. "What are you boys having for lunch?" she said. She had been the waitress there for years. She had been a young girl there and now she was not young any more.

"Today's special is meat loaf, isn't it?" Doc Edwards said.

"Yes, 'Meat loaf for a gray day is the best way,' that's our motto," she said.

Everybody laughed. It was a good joke.

"I'll have some meat loaf," Fred said.

"What about you?" the waitress said. "Meat loaf?"

"Yeah, meat loaf," I said.

"Three meat loaves," the waitress said.

Apple Pie

AFTER LUNCH Doc Edwards had to leave early to go and check on Ron's woman and the new baby to see that they were doing all right.

"See you later," he said.

Fred and I stayed there for a while and drank another cup of coffee at our leisure. Fred put two lumps of watermelon sugar in his coffee.

"How's Margaret doing?" he said. "Have you seen her or heard from her?"

"No," I said. "I told you that this morning."

"She's in pretty bad shape over you and Pauline," Fred said. "She's having a lot of trouble accepting it. I was talking to her brother yesterday. He said she's got a broken heart."

"I can't help that," I said.

"Why are you mad at her?" Fred said. "You don't think she had anything to do with inBOIL just because everybody else does, except Pauline and me?

"There's no proof. It doesn't even make sense in the first place. It was just a coincidence that linked them together. You don't believe she had anything to do with inBOIL, do you?"

"I don't know," I said.

Fred shrugged his shoulders and took a sip of his coffee. The waitress came over and asked us if we wanted a piece of pie for dessert. "We've got some apple pie that really tastes good," she said.

"I'd like a piece of pie," Fred said.

"What about you?"

"No," I said.

Literature

"WELL, I've got to get back to work," Fred said. "The plank press calls. What are you going to do?"

"I think I'll go write," I said. "Work on my book for a while."

"That sounds ambitious," Fred said. "Is the book about weather like the schoolteacher said?"

"No, it's not about weather."

"Good," Fred said. "I wouldn't want to read a book about weather."

"Have you ever read a book?" I said.

"No," Fred said. "I haven't but I don't think I'd want to start by reading one about clouds."

The Way

FRED WENT OFF to the Watermelon Works and I started back to my shack to write, and then I decided not to. I didn't know what to do.

I could go back to iDEATH and talk to Charley about an idea I had or I could go find Pauline and make love to her or I could go to the Statue of Mirrors and sit down there for a while.

That's what I did.

The Statue of Mirrors

EVERYTHING IS REFLECTED in the Statue of Mirrors if you stand there long enough and empty your mind of everything else but the mirrors, and you must be careful not to want anything from the mirrors. They just have to happen.

An hour or so passed as my mind drained out. Some people cannot see anything in the Statue of Mirrors, not even themselves.

Then I could see iDEATH and the town and the Forgotten Works and rivers and fields and the piney woods and the ball park and the Watermelon Works.

I saw Old Chuck on the front porch of iDEATH. He was scratching his head and Charley was in the kitchen buttering himself a slice of toast.

Doc Edwards was walking down the street from Ron's shack and a dog was following behind him, sniffing his footsteps. The dog stopped at one particular footstep and stood there with its tail wagging above the footstep. The dog really liked that one.

The shacks of inBOIL and that gang of his lay now only as ashes by the gate to the Forgotten Works. A bird was looking near the ashes for something. The bird didn't find what it was looking for, got tired and flew away.

I saw Pauline walking through the piney woods up toward

112

my shack. She was carrying a painting with her. It was a surprise for me.

I saw some kids playing baseball in the ball park. One of the kids pitching had a good fast ball and a lot of control. He threw five strikes in a row.

I saw Fred directing his crew in the making of a golden plank of watermelon sugar. He was telling somebody to be careful with his end.

I saw Margaret climbing an apple tree beside her shack. She was crying and had a scarf knotted around her neck. She took the loose end of the scarf and tied it to a branch covered with young apples. She stepped off the branch and then she was standing by herself on the air.

The Grand Old Trout Again

I STOPPED LOOKING into the Statue of Mirrors. I'd seen enough for that day. I sat down on a couch by the river and stared into the water of the deep pool that's there. Margaret was dead.

There was a swirl of water on the surface that cleared the pool all the way down to the bottom, and I saw The Grand Old Trout staring back at me, with the little iDEATH bell hanging from his jaw.

He must have swum upstream from where they were putting the tomb in. That's a long way for an old trout. He must have left just after I did.

The Grand Old Trout did not take his eyes off me. He remained stationary in the water, staring intently at me as he had been doing earlier in the day when he lay by the tomb they were putting in.

There was another swirl of water on the surface of the pool and then I could not see The Grand Old Trout any more. When the pool cleared again, The Grand Old Trout was gone. I stared at the place where he had been in the river. It was empty now like a room.

Getting Fred

I WENT DOWN to the Watermelon Works to see Fred. He was rather surprised to see me down there for the second time that day.

"Hi," he said, looking up from a golden plank that he had been checking out for something. "What's up?"

"It's Margaret," I said.

"Have you seen her?"

"Yes."

"What happened?"

"She's dead. I saw her in the Statue of Mirrors. She hanged herself from an apple tree with her blue scarf."

Fred put the plank down. He bit his lip and ran his hand through his hair. "When did this happen?"

"Just a little while ago. Nobody knows she's dead yet."

Fred shook his head. "I guess we'd better go get her brother."

"Where's he at?"

"He's helping a farmer put a new roof on his barn. We'll go there."

Fred told the crew to knock off for the day. They were quite pleased when Fred told them this. "Thanks, boss," they said.

We left the Watermelon Works with Fred suddenly looking very tired.

The Wind Again

THE GRAY SUN shone feebly. A wind came up and things that could rustle or move in the wind did so all about us as we walked down the road to the barn.

"Why do you think she killed herself?" Fred said. "Why should she do a thing like that? She was so young. So young."

"I don't know," I said. "I don't know why she killed herself."

"It's just terrible," Fred said. "I wish I didn't have to think about it. You haven't the slightest idea, huh? You haven't seen her?"

"No, I was looking into the Statue of Mirrors and she hanged herself there. She's dead now."

Margaret's Brother

MARGARET'S BROTHER was up on the barn roof, nailing blue watermelon shingles down and the farmer was climbing up the ladder, bringing him another bundle of shingles.

Her brother saw us coming up the road and stood up on the barn roof and waved at quite a distance before we got there.

"I don't like this," Fred said.

"Hello, there," her brother yelled.

"What brings you up this way?" the farmer yelled.

We waved back but didn't say anything until we got there.

"Howdy," the farmer said, shaking hands with us. "What are you doing up this way?"

Margaret's brother climbed down the ladder. "Hello," he said and shook our hands and stood there waiting for us to say something. We were strangely quiet and they picked up on it immediately.

Fred pawed at the ground with his boot. He drew a kind of half-circle with his right boot on the ground, and then he erased it with his left boot. This took only a few seconds.

"What's wrong?" the farmer said.

"Yeah, what's wrong?" her brother said.

"It's Margaret," Fred said.

"What's wrong with Margaret?" her brother said. "Tell me."

"She's dead," Fred said.

"How did it happen?"

"She hanged herself."

Margaret's brother stared straight ahead for a little while. His eyes were dim. Nobody said anything. Fred drew another circle in the dust, and then kicked it away.

"It's for the best," Margaret's brother said, finally. "Nobody's to blame. She had a broken heart."

The Wind Again, Again

WE WENT and got the body. The farmer had to stay behind. He said he would have come along but he had to stay and milk his cows. The wind was blowing harder now and a few small things fell down.

Necklace

MARGARET'S BODY was hanging from the apple tree in front of her shack and blowing in the wind. Her neck was at a wrong angle and her face was the color of what we learn to know as death.

Fred climbed up the tree and cut the scarf with his jackknife while Margaret's brother and I lowered her body gently down. He took her body then, and carried it into the shack and lay it down upon the bed.

We stood there.

"Let's take her to iDEATH," Fred said. "That's where she belongs."

Her brother looked relieved for the first time since we had told him of her death.

He went to a large chest by the window and took out a necklace that had small metal trout encircling it. He lifted up her head and fastened the clasp of the necklace. He brushed Margaret's hair out of her eyes.

Then he wrapped her body in a bedspread that had iDEATH crocheted upon it in one of its many and lasting forms. One of her feet was sticking out. The toes looked cold and gently at rest.

Couch

WE TOOK Margaret back to iDEATH. Somehow everybody there had already heard of her death and they were waiting for us. They were out on the front porch.

Pauline ran down the stairs to me. She was very upset and her cheeks were wet with tears. "Why?" she said. "Why?"

I put my arm around her the best I could. "I don't know," I said.

Margaret's brother carried her body up the stairs into iDEATH. Charley opened the door for him. "Here, let me open the door for you."

"Thank you," her brother said. "Where shall I put her?"

"On the couch back in the trout hatchery," Charley said. "That's where we put our dead."

"I don't remember the way," her brother said. "I haven't been here for a long time."

"I'll show you. Follow me," Charley said.

"Thank you."

They went off to the trout hatchery. Fred went with them and so did Old Chuck and Al and Bill. I stayed behind with my arm around Pauline. She was still crying. I guess she really liked Margaret.

Tomorrow

PAULINE AND I went down for a walk by the river in the living room. It was now nearing sundown. Tomorrow the sun would be black, soundless. The night would continue but the stars would not shine and it would be warm like day and everything would be without sound.

"This is horrible," Pauline said. "I feel so bad. Why did she kill herself? Was it my fault for loving you?"

"No," I said. "It was nobody's fault. Just one of those things."

"We were such good friends. We were like sisters. I'd hate to think it was my fault."

"Don't," I said.

Carrots

DINNER THAT NIGHT was a quiet affair at iDEATH. Margaret's brother stayed and had dinner with us. Charley invited him.

Al cooked up a mess of carrots again. He broiled them with mushrooms and a sauce made from watermelon sugar and spices. There was hot bread fresh from the oven and sweet butter and glasses of ice-cold milk.

About halfway through dinner, Fred started to say something that looked as if it were important, but then he changed his mind and went back to eating his carrots.

Margaret's Room

AFTER DINNER everybody went into the living room and it was decided to hold the funeral tomorrow morning, even though it would be dark and there would be no sound and everything would have to be done in silence.

"If it's all right with you," Charley said to Margaret's brother. "She'll be buried in that tomb we've been working on. They finished it this afternoon."

"That would be perfect," her brother said.

"It will be dark and there will be no sound, but I think we can take care of everything."

"Yeah," her brother said.

"Fred, will you go and tell the people in the town about the funeral? Some of them might want to go. Also alert the Tomb Crew about the funeral. And see if you can find some flowers."

"Sure, Charley. I'll take care of it."

"It's our custom to brick up the rooms of those who lived here when they die," Charley said.

"What does that mean?" Margaret's brother said.

"We put bricks across the door and close the room forever."

"That sounds all right."

Bricks

PAULINE AND Margaret's brother and Charley and Bill, he had the bricks, and I went to Margaret's room. Charley opened the door.

Pauline was carrying a lantern. She put it down on Margaret's table and lit the lantern that was there with a long watermelon match.

There were now two lights.

The room was filled with things from the Forgotten Works. Every place you looked there was something forgotten that was piled on another forgotten thing.

Charley shook his head. "A lot of forgotten things in here. We don't even know what most of the things are," he said to nobody.

Margaret's brother sighed.

"Is there anything you want to take with you?" Charley said.

Her brother looked all around the room very carefully and very sadly and then shook his head, too. "No, brick it all up."

We stepped outside and Bill started putting the bricks in place. We watched for a little while. There were tears in Pauline's eyes.

"Please spend the night with us," Charley said.

"Thank you," Margaret's brother said.

"I'll show you to your room. Good night," Charley said to us. He went off with her brother. He was saying something to him.

"Let's go, Pauline," I said.

"All right, honey."

"I think you'd better sleep with me tonight."

"Yes," she said.

We left Bill putting the bricks in place. They were watermelon bricks made from black, soundless sugar. They made no sound as he worked with them. They would seal off the forgotten things forever.

My Room

PAULINE AND I went to my room. We took off our clothes and got into bed. She took off her clothes first and I watched.

"Are you going to blow the lantern out?" she said, leaning forward as I got into bed last.

She did not have any covers up over her breasts. The nipples were hard. They were almost the same color as her lips. They looked beautiful in the lantern light. Her eyes were red from crying. She looked very tired.

"No," I said.

She put her head back on the pillow and smiled ever so faintly. Her smile was like the color of her nipples.

"No," I said.

The Girl with the Lantern Again

AFTER WHILE I let Pauline go to sleep, but then I had my usual trouble sleeping. She was warm and sweet-smelling beside me. Her body called me to sleep as if it were a band of trumpets. I lay there for a long time before I got up and went for one of the walks I take at night.

I stood there with my clothes on, watching Pauline sleep. Strange, how well Pauline has slept since we have been going steady together, for Pauline was the girl who went for the long walks at night, carrying the lantern. Pauline was the girl I wondered so much about, walking up and down the roads, stopping at this place, this bridge, this river, these trees in the piney woods.

Her hair is blonde and now she is asleep.

After we started going steady she stopped her long walks at night, but I still continue mine. It suits me to take these long walks at night.

Margaret Again, Again, Again, Again, Again

I WENT TO THE TROUT HATCHERY and stood there staring at the cold undelightful body now of Margaret. She lay upon the couch and there were lanterns all around. The trout had trouble sleeping.

There were some fingerlings darting around in a tray that had a lantern by the edge of it, illuminating Margaret's face. I stared at the fingerlings for a long time, hours passed, until they went to sleep. They were now like Margaret.

Good Ham

WE WOKE UP an hour or so before sunrise and had an early breakfast. When the sun came up over the edge of our world, the darkness would continue and there would be no sound today. Our voices would be gone. If you dropped something, there would be no sound. The rivers would be silent.

"It's going to be a long day," Pauline said, as she put on her dress, pulling it over her long smooth neck.

We had ham and eggs, hashbrowns and toast. Pauline cooked breakfast and I offered to help her. "Is there anything I can do?" I said.

"No," she said. "I've got everything under control but thanks for the offer."

"You're welcome."

We all had breakfast together, including Margaret's brother. He sat next to Charley.

"This is good ham," Fred said.

"We'll hold the funeral later on in the morning," Charley said. "Everybody knows what they have to do and we can write notes if anything out of the ordinary comes up. We just have a few moments of sound left."

"Ummmm—good ham," Fred said.

Sunrise

PAULINE AND I were in the kitchen talking when the sun came up. She was washing the dishes and I was drying them. I was drying a frying pan and she was washing the coffee cups.

"I feel a little bit better today," she said.

"Good," I said.

"How did I sleep last night?"

"Like a top."

"I had a bad dream. I hope I didn't wake you up."

"No."

"The shock yesterday was something. I don't know. I just didn't expect things to turn out this way, but they have, and I guess there's nothing we can do about it."

"That's right," I said. "Just take things the way they happen."

Pauline turned toward me and said, "I guess the funeral will—"

Escutcheon

MARGARET WAS DRESSED in death robes made from watermelon sugar and adorned with beads of foxfire, so that the light would shine forever from her tomb at night and on the black, soundless days. This one.

She had been prepared now for the tomb. We moved in lanterns and silence about iDEATH, waiting for the townspeople to come.

They came. Thirty or forty arrived, including the editor of the newspaper. It is published once a year. The schoolteacher and Doc Edwards were there and then we started the funeral.

Margaret was carried on the Escutcheon we use for the dead, made from pine ornamented with glass and little distant stones.

Everybody had torches and lanterns and we carried her body out of the trout hatchery and through the living room and out the door and across the porch and down the steps of iDEATH.

Sunny Morning

THE PROCESSION moved slowly and in total silence down the road to the new tomb that now belonged to Margaret, the one I had watched them building yesterday, putting the finishing touches on for Margaret. It was getting warm as the sun climbed higher in the sky. There was not even the sound of our footsteps or anything.

The Tomb Crew

THE TOMB CREW was waiting for us. They still had the Shaft in place and they started the pump going when they saw us coming.

We turned the body over to them and they went about putting it in the tomb. They've had a lot of experience doing that. They carried her body down the Shaft and put it in the tomb. They closed the glass door and started to seal it up.

Pauline, Charley, Fred, Old Chuck and I stood there together in a little group and watched them. Pauline took my arm. Margaret's brother came over and joined us.

After the Tomb Crew had sealed the door, they turned the pump off and removed the hose from the Shaft.

Then they harnessed up some horses with ropes to the two pulleys that were hanging from the Shaft Gallows. Ropes went from the Shaft Gallows to hooks in the Shaft itself.

That's how they get the Shaft out.

The horses strained forward and the Shaft was pulled free from the bottom of the river and was lifted up onto the shore and was now half-hanging from the Shaft Gallows.

The Tomb Crew and their horses looked tired. Everything was done in total silence. Not a sound came from the horses or the men or the Shaft or the river or the people watching.

We saw the light shining up from Margaret, the light that

came from the foxfire upon her robes. We took flowers and threw them upstream above her tomb.

The flowers drifted down over the light coming from her: roses and daffodils and poppies and bluebells floated on by.

The Dance

IT IS A CUSTOM HERE to hold a dance in the trout hatchery after a funeral. Everybody comes and there's a good band and much dancing goes on. We all like to waltz.

After the funeral we went back to iDEATH and prepared for the dance. Party decorations were put up in the hatchery and refreshments were prepared for the dance.

Everybody got ready in silence. Charley put on some new overalls. Fred spent half an hour combing his hair and Pauline put on high heel shoes.

We could not start the party until there was sound, so that the musical instruments would work and we could work with them in our own style, mostly waltzing.

Cooks Together

PAULINE AND Al together cooked an early dinner that we had late in the afternoon. It was very hot outside, so they prepared something light. They made a potato salad that somehow ended up having a lot of carrots in it.

Their Instruments Playing

PEOPLE FROM THE TOWN began arriving for the dance about half an hour before sundown. We took their Mackinaws and hats and showed them into the trout hatchery.

Everybody seemed to be in fairly good spirits. The musicians took out their instruments and waited for the sun to go down.

It would only be a few moments now. We all waited patiently. The room glowed with lanterns. The trout swam back and forth in their trays and ponds. We would dance around them.

Pauline looked very pretty. Charley's new overalls looked good. I don't know why Fred's hair looked as if he hadn't combed it at all.

The musicians were poised with their instruments. They were ready to go. It would only be a few seconds now, I wrote.

This novel was started May 13, 1964 in a house at Bolinas, California, and was finished July 19, 1964 in the front room at 123 Beaver Street, San Francisco, California. This novel is for Don Allen, Joanne Kyger and Michael McClure.